A CHILDHOOD STORY OF WASHINGTON SIMPSON STYLES SR.

Pop Pop
and the
Red Wagon

BY: DENISE STYLES & SARAI STYLES

ISBN: 978-1-7355915-8-2 (paperback)

978-1-7355915-9-9 (hardcover)

First Edition Book, July 2022

Book cover design, illustration, editing, and interior layout by

www.1000storybooks.com

Dedication

This book is dedicated to Washington Simpson Styles Sr.

12/17/1917 - 12/2/2020

It was a hot summer day. The sun was beaming down on us as we played tag, rode on bikes, played hopscotch, and just ran around in the sun.

5

Everyone met up at Aunt Dee's house on days like this. In our family, she is known as "Aunt Dee," even though her name is Denise. Aunt Dee had the best yard, the best snacks, and the best ice pops, but the best part about Aunt Dee's house was that we always knew Pop Pop was in his room, ready to tell us stories when we got tired of running around.

7

As it started to get dark, we all rushed inside to play more games and have more fun.

(Inside the house) I walked up the stairs while my cousins followed behind me. Pop Pop's door was cracked open, and the light was on inside.

"Can I go to Pop Pop's room?" I asked Aunt Dee.

"Of course, you can. Just knock first," said Aunt Dee.

"Okay!"

I peeked in the little crack and noticed Pop Pop was deep in his Bible.

"Can I come in?" I whispered.

"Yeah, come on in," Pop Pop said, smiling up at me.

17

"What are you reading?" I asked, wandering into the room.

"My favorite story in the Bible. The story of Abraham."

"Can you tell me one of your stories from when you were a little boy?" I asked.

"Sure I can!" Pop Pop gave a big smile.

"One second!" I ran into the living room and yelled, "Pop Pop is telling a story!"

21

All my cousins came running behind me into Pop Pop's room.

"We are ready!" I said, as we all found a spot. Some of us were on the floor, on his bed, and even on his lap.

23

"I have the perfect story for y'all," Pop Pop said. "When I was six years old, I wanted a red wagon…Now I knew that I could not have that red wagon, because times were tough, and money did not grow on trees." Pop-pop closed his eyes, then rubbed his hand across his face.

"Pop Pop, what did you want to do if you had a red wagon?" I asked.

25

"I can see it now: the big, bright red wagon carrying my heavy books for school. I can see the big black wheels going around and around. I can see the long wooden handle that I would hold tight as I strolled along to school," Pop Pop said.

"If I had that red wagon, my cousin Estell and I would take turns sitting in the wagon while the others pulled. When it was my turn to pull, I would run as fast as I could. Estell would have her hands up high while the hot summer air blew on our faces."

29

"If I had that red wagon, I would collect rocks with my cousin Duck. Duck and I would go down to the lake and skip rocks all day long. We would see who could throw the rocks the farthest."

"If I had that red wagon, I could go to the garden in the backyard with my friend May. May and I loved to grow fruits, vegetables, and flowers. When it was time to pick the fruits, May and I could put all the fruits into the wagon and bring it into the house. We could even surprise my mom with flowers."

"If I had that red wagon, I could help my mom bring in groceries. My mom is your great-great-grandmother. Her name was Eva. When my mother and I had to walk to the store, I could bring my wagon so she did not have to carry anything. She could walk down the road empty-handed while singing songs."

"If I had that red wagon, I would clean up all my toys. My mom never liked it when my toys were all over the place, so I could load up my wagon and put my toys back into my toy box."

"The best thing I could have done with that red wagon was to walk with my dad and carry his Bibles. My dad's name was Isaiah. He loved to travel and preach the word of God. He had to travel long distances, and sometimes I would go with him. All of those heavy Bibles could go into my wagon, and I could walk beside my father."

"Wow, I loved that story, Pop Pop!" I said. "If I had a red wagon, I would carry all my board games so we could play them wherever we go."

We all gave Pop Pop a big hug and thanked him for telling us his childhood story.

Pop Pop celebrated his birthday this year. He turned 100 years old. On Christmas, my dad, Shamar Styles, gifted Pop Pop the red wagon he always wanted. I've never seen him smile so big!

DENISE STYLES

Denise Styles is a daughter, a mother of two sons, a grandmother of four granddaughters, a sister, a first-time author, and a supportive friend all in one. Her sons have made her who she is today, even though they may not know it. Those who are closest to her describe her as a woman of valor, and class. Denise attributes a lot of her redeemable qualities to her father, Washington Simpson Styles Sr., who she describes as an incredibly hardworking, helpful, and giving man. Denise is currently in the crafting business, after working as an operator at General Motors for twenty-five years. Her creativity and dedication have helped her flourish in her career, while her personability and compassionate attitude has helped her maintain strong relationships with people she cares for. Simply put, her positive attributes know no limits. She is known for how strong, beautiful, funny, dependable, and powerful she is—and that does not even scratch the surface of how amazing she truly is.

SARAI STYLES

Sarai Styles is a fourteen year-old author of The Alphabet Book in English and French, co-author of a children's book entitled, Mommy, Why am I Different?, and is now a co-author of Pop Pop and the Red Wagon. Sarai Styles is a young black girl who wants to create books that celebrate diversity, community, self-esteem empowerment, and positive relationship development at home and school. Sarai Styles is excited to share one of her great-grandfather's childhood stories.

Lightning Source UK Ltd.
Milton Keynes UK
UKHW050910020822
406704UK00002B/53

* 9 7 8 1 7 3 5 5 9 1 5 9 9 *